I0610324

Mary T. Rush

Ocean City, N.J.

guide book and directory

Mary T. Rush

Ocean City, N.J.
guide book and directory

ISBN/EAN: 9783337316709

Printed in Europe, USA, Canada, Australia, Japan

Cover: Foto ©Andreas Hilbeck / pixelio.de

More available books at **www.hansebooks.com**

Giant Finback or Rorqual Whale, came ashore at Ocean City October 8, 1891; 68 feet long.

OCEAN CITY

Guide Book and Directory

CONTAINING

A List of Permanent and Temporary Residents, Street Directory,
Societies, Religious Services, Historical and Biographical
Sketches, Wrecks, etc., Railroad and Steam-
boat Time-Tables, etc.

PUBLISHED BY
MRS. J. S. RUSH.

" The ocean old,
    Centuries old,
Strong as youth and as uncontrolled,
Paces restless to and fro,
Up and down the sands of gold.
His beating heart is not at rest;
    And far and wide,
    With ceaseless flow,
    His beard of snow,
Heaves with the heaving of his breast."

HON. SIMON LAKE.

REV. F. B. LAKE.

REV. S. W. LAKE.

REV. J. F. LAKE.

PREFACE.

Believing that Ocean City is destined to rank among the first of summer resorts of the New Jersey coast, and in response to a desire frequently expressed by our citizens and visitors, we have endeavored to set forth in as compact form as possible, many of its most interesting and important features.

As this is the first effort made in the direction of a Guide Book and Directory, the compilation has been tedious and difficult, and there may be errors and omissions, which we ask our readers to overlook. The constantly changing population of a seaside resort renders accuracy almost impossible except for a short period. We believe, however, the book to be so complete as to be of great advantage to our citizens, our summer residents and transient guests. The demand has already secured for it a large circulation.

We are indebted for information contained in the historical sketches to the marine official records of the coast, the " Historical Collections" of the state, and to the older residents, the Life Guards, Sailors and Fishermen of Southern New Jersey.

Much credit is due the talented artist W. Edwards, late of Lynchburg, Va., for the fine views photographed for the work, and the Crosscup & West Engraving Co., Philadelphia, for the handsome engravings on copper-plate.

Officers.

Mayor, G. P. Moore, office, 835 Asbury ave.

COUNCIL.

J. Conver, office, 443 West ave.
N. Corson, office, 653 Asbury ave.
F. P. Canfield, office, W. cor. Sixth st. and Asbury ave.
J. C. Steelman, office, 1259 Asbury ave.

Clerk, H. B. Adams, office, E. cor. Eighth and West.
Collector and Treasurer, H. G. Steelman, 705 Asbury ave.
Assessor, R. Ludlam, 823 Asbury ave.
Marshal, H. Conver, 711 Asbury ave.
Coroner, A. E. Cox, S. cor. Eighth st. and Asbury ave.
Freeholder, W. Lake, N. cor. Fourth st. and Central ave.

BOARD OF HEALTH.

President, J. S. Waggoner, 731 Asbury ave.
C. A. Campbell, 813 Asbury ave.
S. Schurch, S. cor. Seventh st. and Asbury ave.
P. Murdock, 805 Asbury ave.
J. C. Steelman, 1259 Asbury ave.

WATER DEPARTMENT.

President, Rev. E. B. Lake.

REV. J. B. GRAW, D.D.,
President Ocean City Association.

First M. E. Church,

Eight st. and Central ave.   Rev. W. A. Massey, Pastor.

Services—10.30 A.M., 8.00 P.M.

Sunday School, 2.30 P.M.   G. P. Moore, Supt.

Christian Endeavor, 6.30 P.M.   Miss M. Lake, President.

Devotional Meetings, Tues., Wed., Thurs., Fri., 7.30 P.M.

Ladies' Aid Society.   Mrs. D. W. Bartine, President.

Auditorium, Camp Ground.

Camp Meeting and other religious services during summer months.

Woman's Christian Temperance Union.

Miss Alice Canfield, President.

Building Loan Association.

Officers—Pres., G. P. Moore; Sec., Wm. Lake; Treas., R. H. Thorn.

Directors—H. Steelman, G. Ang, S. Miller, G. O. Adams, J. Brower, S. Sampson.

Secret Societies.

Junior Order United American Mechanics.   Knights of Pythias.

Brass Band.

H. G. Steelman, Leader.

Life-Saving Stations.

1. Ocean City, Capt. J. S. Willets.
2. Peck's Beach, Capt. L. Godfrey.
3. Corson's Inlet, Capt. C. D. Stephens.

Directory.

A

Adams H B, real estate, 411 Fifth st; office, E cor Eighth st and West ave.

Adams J T, "Traymore," S cor Ninth st and Wesley ave.

Adams W W, stone mason, Asbury ave, bel Tenth st.

Adams G O, stone mason, 1057 West ave.

Allen E, Asbury ave abv Fourth st, also Frankford, Pa.

Allen & Hughes, 444 Asbury ave.

Atwood P C J, 1233 Central ave, also Phila, Pa.

B

Bamford A E Mrs, 443 Asbury ave, also Phila, Pa.

Baner M, W cor Sixth st and Ocean ave, also Phila, Pa.

Barrows A D, N cor Thirty-fourth st and Asbury ave.

Barber W A, Ocean City, Manager Atlantic Steamboat Co.

Bartine D W, M D, 717 Wesley ave.

Bartine W, 717 Wesley ave.

Barnett B G, Asbury ave abv First st, also Camden, N J.

Barnhurst W, 1612 Asbury ave, also Phila, Pa.

Bardsley S, 1204 Central ave, also Phila, Pa.

Bassett S, 930 Wesley ave, also Bridgeton, N J.

Bebee S, Ocean ave abv Fourth st, also Frankford, Pa.

Beriners A Mrs, "Atlantic Villa," N cor Seventh st and Ocean ave, also Phila, Pa.

Bethany S S, "Ocean Rest," N cor Thirty-second st and Wesley ave, also Phila, Pa.

Bennett J, hauling, W cor Eighth st and Asbury ave.

MAYOR G. P. MOORE.

MAYOR MOORE'S RESIDENCE.

Bingham B C, Simpson ave bel First st, also Camden, N J.

Borgner H C, "Allaire," S cor Sixth st and Central ave, also Lebanon, Pa.

Borie C, Asbury ave abv First st, also Frankford, Pa.

Boyle W E Mrs, 429 Wesley ave.

Breckley G N Capt Sr, Central ave bel 8th st, also Washington, D C.

Breckley G N Jr, painter, 310 Fourth st.

Briggs J, stone mason, 1127 West ave.

Brower J, painter, store Asbury ave abv Seventh st, res S cor Third st and Central ave.

Brower Jos, S cor Third st and Central ave.

Brown T J, Central ave abv First st, also Atlantic City, N J.

Bryan J T, 1249 Asbury ave, also Phila, Pa.

Brucker E, E cor Tenth st and Central ave, also Phila, Pa.

Bourgeois E A, rest 808 Asbury ave, res S cor Ninth st and Central ave.

Bourgeois G A, carpenter, 420 Central ave.

Burroughs R, painter, E cor Sixth st and Asbury ave.

Burley Jos, " Vandalia House," Central ave abv Eighth st.

Burley A, carpenter, W cor Fourteenth st and West ave.

Burt J, Wesley ave bel Ninth st, also Bridgeton, N J.

Burrell W H Rev, Ocean City, N J, also 43 Cooper st, Camden, N J.

Burnley C W Rev, 924 Wesley ave, also Williamsport, Pa.

C

Campbell C A, store and res 813 Asbury ave.

Canfield J T Rev, " Illinois," W cor Sixth st and Asbury ave.

Canfield H D, " Illinois," W cor Sixth st and Asbury ave. See adv.

Canfield F P, councilman, "Illinois," W cor Sixth st and Asbury ave.

Carson J R, 1205 Central ave, also Camden, N J.

Carhart S, painter, W cor Twelfth st and Asbury ave.

Champion F E, rest and res N cor Seventh st and Asbury ave.

Champion M, teamster, 405 Seventh st.

Champion I, carousel, res Asbury ave abv Seventh st.

Champion J, builder, "Sea Breeze," 704 Central ave.

Champion Q, painter, "Sea Breeze," 704 Central ave.

Chance J C, Asbury ave abv First st, also Vineland, N J.
Chew W, carpenter, West ave abv Thirteenth st.
Christ A E Mrs, Central ave bel Sixth st, also Phila, Pa.
Clark J, E cor Seventeenth st and West ave, also May's Landing, N J.
Clawell D, N cor Seventeenth st and Asbury ave, also Phila, Pa.
Clelland M C, 822 Wesley ave, also Phila, Pa.
Clifton J, plasterer, Simpson ave bel Second st.
Collins S, 1408 West ave, also Seaville, N J.
Colver A H, "The Emmett," W cor Eighth st and Central ave.
Conver J, councilman, store 623 Asbury ave, res 443 West ave.
Conver H L, store and res 711 Asbury ave.
Corson M, life guard, 833 Asbury ave.
Corson N, councilman, 653 Asbury ave.
Corson Y, store and res 721 Asbury ave.
Corson O, painter, 721 Asbury ave.
Corson J I Rev, N cor 5th st and Central ave, also Bargaintown, N J.
Corson F R, M D, N cor 11th st and Central ave, also Merchantville.
Corson J M, 1632 Central ave, also Palermo, N J.
Cowperthwait S S E, 1220 Central ave, also Camden, N J.
Cotton A, 433 Asbury ave, also Frackville, Pa.
Cox A E, "Wesley House," W cor Eighth st and Wesley ave.
Cox L, machinist, "Wesley House," W cor Eighth st and Wesley ave.
Coxey J C, E cor Fourteenth st and Asbury ave, also Camden, N J.
Cronin W D, plasterer, "Dolphin," 1046 Asbury ave.
Currey W B, Central ave abv Fifth st, also Phila, Pa.

D

Davis J H, Atlantic ave bel Fourth st, also Phila, Pa.
Davis W A, M D, N cor First st and Central ave, also Camden, N J.
Davis N, M D, E cor First st and Asbury ave, also Camden, N J.
Davis J T, N cor First st and Asbury ave, also Camden, N J.
Demaris A, hackman, E cor Twelfth st and West ave.
Dixon J, Central ave abv Fourth st, also Phila.
Dobbins G L Rev, 922 Wesley ave, also N J Conf.
Doughty C, 431 Asbury ave, also Atlantic City, N J.
Downs J S, "Perennial," 810 Central ave.

EX-MAYOR J. F. PRYOR, M.D.

E

Edowes T, "Home Cottage," 1414 Asbury ave, also Phila, Pa.
Edwards C E, D D S, 809 Wesley ave, also Haddonfield, N J.
Elliot W R, Central ave abv Third st, also Frankford, Pa.
Elwell W H, Sta Agt W J R R, res S cor 8th st and Asbury ave.
Emerson W D, 1606 Asbury ave, also Phila, Pa.
English E B, builder, 915 Asbury ave.
English S Mrs, 915 Asbury ave.
English J A, 629 Central ave, also Phila, Pa.
Esher E H, 1620 Asbury ave, also Phila, Pa.
Eves Misses, 708 Central ave, also Media, Pa.

F

Fenstermacher G, Wesley ave abv Eighth st, also Phila, Pa.
Fletcher M Miss, 117 Asbury ave.
Fanelli T, laborer, 328 West ave.
Foulds H, W cor Fourth st and Ocean ave, also Phila, Pa.
Fisher R, real estate, N cor Seventh st and Wesley ave.

G

Gandy J G, store 745 Asbury ave, res W cor 8th st and Asbury ave.
Gandy O M, painter, W cor Eighth st and Asbury ave.
Garland W G, 640 Central ave, also Phila, Pa.
Garwood S P, carpenter, 418 Wesley ave.
Garrison W R, life guard, 831 Asbury ave.
Garrison S O Rev, 1658 Central ave, also Vineland, N J.
Gerlach H, cor Sixteenth st and Asbury ave, also Phila, Pa.
Gilbert A G, painter, Asbury ave abv Third st.
Glickert R, Asbury ave bel Fourteenth st, also Phila, Pa.
Godfrey W, bath-house, res 629 Asbury ave.
Graham F R, M D, W cor 10th st and Wesley ave, also Chester, Pa.
Griffith A E Mrs, M D, W cor 16th st and Central ave, also Phila.
Griffith L R Mrs, W cor Seventh st and Central ave, also Phila, Pa.

H

Hagle W, Asbury ave bel Sixteenth st, also Phila, Pa.

Haines H, S cor Ninth st and Wesley ave, also Mt. Ephraim, N J.

Hand J F, builder, 721 Central ave.

Hayes N, carpenter, 825 Asbury ave.

Headley L, carpenter, 829 Asbury ave.

Heisler H Miss, "Aldine," Wesley ave abv 9th, also Mt. Holly, N J.

Henderson J C Capt, 447 West ave.

Hess U Y, teamster, 1224 Asbury ave.

Hillman J P, Asbury ave bel Twelfth st, also Camden, N J.

Hickey D W, Cond W J R R, Asbury ave abv Eighth st.

Hoffman B, carpenter, 1241 Asbury ave.

Houck W Capt, Wesley ave abv Sixth st.

Huckle W Rev, 602 Wesley ave, also New York.

Hudson D, Haven ave abv Second, also Millville, N J.

Hunter T, Ocean ave abv Second st, also Phœnixville, Pa.

Hutchinson J H Rev, "Aldine," Wesley ave abv 9th st, also N J Conf.

Hyde Mrs, "Lafayette," W cor 13th st and Central ave, also Vineland.

I

Ingersoll B, carpenter, Central ave bel Sixth st.

J

Jeffries J H Capt, 347 West ave.

Jeffries J B Capt, 347 West ave.

Jeffries M, pound-keeper, 347 West ave.

Jeffries Geo Capt, 347 West ave.

Jackson M Mrs, laundress, 326 West ave.

Jones W, 437 Asbury ave, also Phila, Pa.

Joseph A Mrs, 408 Wesley ave, also Phila, Pa.

K

Kendrick J R, 820 Wesley ave, also Phila, Pa.

King C, Asbury ave bel Fourth st.

Krouse G, 305 Central ave, also Phila, Pa.

Kynett A G Rev, 1233 Central ave, also Phila Conf.

Kynett H H, M D, 1225 Central ave, also Phila, Pa.

Kynett A J Rev, 1229 Central ave, also Phila, Pa.

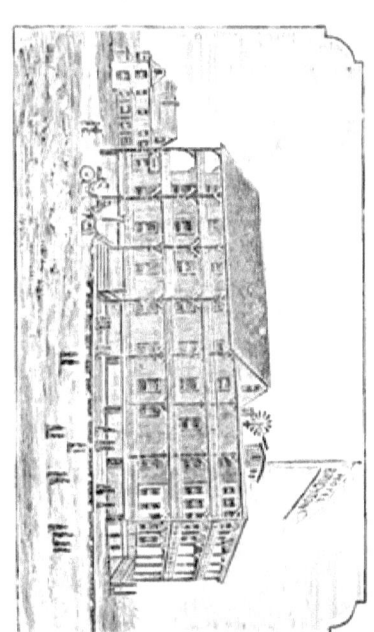

HOTEL BRIGHTON.

L

Lake W, real estate, N cor Fourth st and Central ave.

Lake D E, builder, 1628 Asbury ave.

Lake M Capt, 450 West ave.

Lake F B Rev, real estate, E cor Fifth st and Wesley ave.

Lake H Mrs, 413 Fifth st.

Lake S W Rev, Ocean City, also N J Conf.

Lake J E Rev, Ocean City, also N J Conf.

Lake J T, Asbury ave bel Fourteenth st, also Pleasantville, N J.

Lee I Capt, 939 Asbury ave.

Lennig G G, Simpson ave bel First st, also Phila, Pa.

Lee J W, store and res Asbury ave bel Seventh st.

Lewallen J, barber, 711 Asbury ave.

Linn J, 324 Central ave, also Phila, Pa.

Loder E B, S cor Twelfth st and Central ave, also Phila, Pa.

Lonobough J C, 1212 Central ave, also Phila, Pa.

Ludlam R, assessor, 823 Asbury ave.

M

Mahoney D, 1643 West ave, also Phila.

Mapps W R, 1416 Asbury ave, also Long Branch, N J.

Marter H H, 934 Asbury ave, also Camden, N J.

Massey W A Rev, 716 Asbury ave, also N J Conf.

Marshall A, 712 Ocean ave, also Phila, Pa.

Matthews C, Ocean City, also Phila, Pa.

McAllister J C, Asbury ave abv First st, also Phila, Pa.

McAleese J, 1409 Asbury ave.

McGuire J H, Wesley ave abv Eighth st, also Phila, Pa.

Miller P Capt, 726 Asbury ave.

Miller W Capt, 726 Asbury ave.

Miller S B, carpenter, 733 Central ave.

Miller C G, engineer W J R R, 1640 Asbury ave.

Moore G P, mayor, 835 Asbury ave.

Moore E, painter, 835 Asbury ave.

Moore M, slate-roofer, 835 Asbury ave.

Morey J K, carpenter, Central ave bel Eighth st.
Morris, A Mrs, 404 Asbury ave.
Morris J B, fisherman, 727 West ave.
Morris R Mrs, store and res 714 Asbury ave.
Muir D S, cor Fourth st and Wesley ave, also Phila, Pa.
Murdock J, 215 Asbury ave.
Murdock P, 806 Asbury ave.
Myers C Esq, N cor Eighth st and Wesley ave.

N

Newkirk B, expressman, S cor Fourth st and Asbury ave.
Nelson A, W J R R, 717 Asbury ave, "Ocean City House."
Noble G N Mrs, 722 Asbury ave.
Newcomb H O, Wesley ave bel Ninth st.

P

Palen G E, M D, 825 Wesley ave, also Phila, Pa.
Paxson Misses, W cor Sixth st and Wesley ave, also Phila, Pa.
Pierce O, Ocean City, also Phila, Pa.
Price J T, "Ocean City House," 717 Asbury ave.
Price B D, Atlantic ave abv Fourth st, also Phila, Pa.
Pryor J E, M D, E cor Eighth st and Asbury ave.

R

Ranck A B Mrs, "Allaire," S cor Sixth st and Central ave.
Raney A W Mrs, 409 Fifth st, also Frankford, Pa.
Rapp R, Central ave abv First st, also Phila, Pa.
Rapp J V R, Central ave abv First st, also Phila, Pa.
Rapp F, store and res 756 Asbury ave, also Phila, Pa.
Radcliff J Y, 749 Asbury ave, also Phila, Pa.
Reinhart H, engineer W J R R, 917 Asbury ave.
Reed J, Asbury ave abv Fourteenth st, also Camden, N J.
Rice E L, 1213 Asbury ave, also Bridgeton, N J.
Risley L Capt, W cor Seventh st and Central ave.
Risley W Capt, Asbury ave abv Fourth st.
Risley D Capt, 711 Central ave.

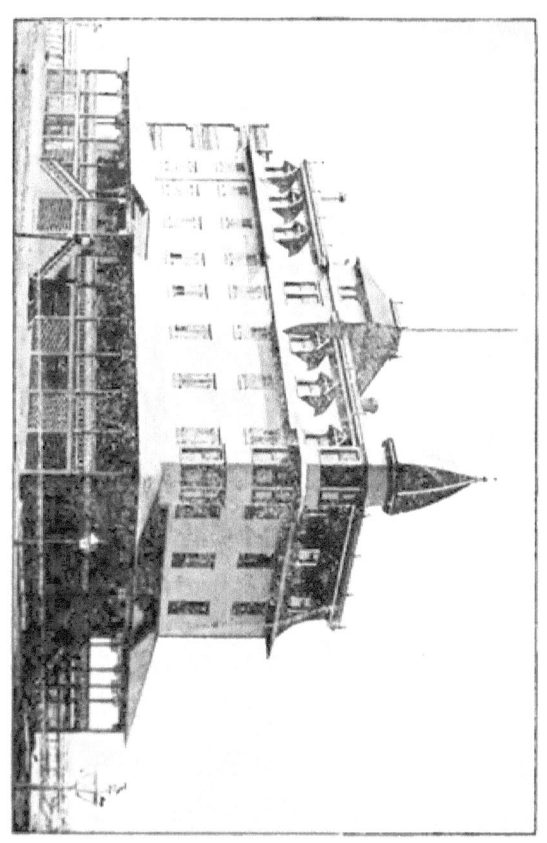

THE TRAYMORE.

Robinson J, 726 Asbury ave.

Robinson R C, office 744 Asbury ave, res 721 Asbury ave.

Roberts Mrs, M D, 604 Wesley ave, also New York.

Rush J S, painter, office E cor Ninth st and Asbury ave, res 219 Wesley ave.

S

Salter J G, S cor Fourteenth st and Asbury ave, also Phila, Pa.

Sampson S B, builder, 305 Fourth st.

Sampson D, tinsmith, Asbury ave abv Fourth st.

Sanderlin B H, Wesley ave bel Eighth st, also Phila, Pa.

Schenck E Mrs, 656 West ave, also Millville, N J.

Schermerhorn C H, 1237 Central ave, also Phila, Pa.

Schuff J, baker, W cor Asbury ave and Seventh st.

Schurch S, "Bellevue," S cor Asbury ave and Seventh st

Schmitt F, E cor Tenth st and Asbury ave, also Phila, Pa.

Schultz H G, Asbury ave bel Sixteenth st, also Phila, Pa.

Scull J C, carpenter, 727 Asbury ave.

Scull A D, builder, Central ave abv Seventh st.

Shaw T, E cor Fifth st and Central ave, also Phila, Pa.

Sharp A D, hackman, 110 Asbury ave.

Sharp C B, hackman, 110 Asbury ave.

Sharp E J, carpenter, 110 Asbury ave.

Sharp W, carpenter, West ave abv Second st.

Sheets S, painter, 825 Asbury ave.

Shriver W, 1221 Asbury ave, also Phila, Pa.

Sipler M H Miss, 708 Asbury ave.

Smith L S, store and res 1140 Asbury ave.

Smith J W, butcher, 644 Central ave.

Smith B R, painter, store Asbury ave bel 6th st, res 1059 West ave.

Smith F, milkman, Asbury ave bel Third st.

Smith E, Asbury ave abv Fourth st, also English Creek, N J.

Smith E, 1447 Asbury ave, also Phila, Pa.

Smith H D, 1209 Central ave, also Phila, Pa.

Somers E Capt, 424 West ave.

Snyder F, store and res Asbury ave abv Eighth st.

Sooy R R, "Brighton," Seventh st and Ocean ave, also Phila, Pa.
Sooy N, West ave bel Fourth st, also Phila, Pa.
Stewart W C, 626 Central ave, also Phila, Pa.
Steelman H, store and res N cor Fourth st and Asbury ave.
Steelman H G, store 705 Asbury ave, res 420 Central ave.
Steelman J C, councilman, 1259 Asbury ave.
Steelman R, "Sea Breeze," 704 Central ave.
Steelman M Mrs, 911 Asbury ave.
Still J, Asbury ave abv Ninth st.
Still L W, Asbury ave abv Ninth st.
Stites R B, lumber, 759 Asbury ave.
Stonehill W, stone mason, 1159 Asbury ave.
Sutton H C, baggage master W J R R, Central ave bel Eighth st.

T

Thatcher J W, W cor Thirteenth st and Asbury ave, also Phila, Pa.
Thatcher J, M D, 728 Ocean ave, also Phila, Pa.
Thegan W, Central ave abv First st, also Camden, N J.
Thomas L R Prof, Wesley ave abv Eighth st.
Thomas A B, S cor Fifteenth st and Asbury ave, also Phila, Pa.
Thomas J, 1228 Asbury ave, also Bridgeton, N J.
Thompson R, Simpson ave bel First st, also Phila, Pa.
Thorn R H, store and res S cor Eighth st and Asbury ave.
Tilton C M, rest and res Bay ave abv Fourth st.
Tweedale S Rev, Asbury ave bel Fourteenth st, also Frankford, Pa.
Turpin J B Rev, Asbury ave bel Fourteenth st, also Gloucester, N J.
Tuttle C P, D D S, Asbury ave abv First st, also Phila, Pa.'

V

Voss J, carpenter, 730 Asbury ave.
Vangilder E Mrs, 1419 Asbury ave, also Petersburg, N J.

W

Waggoner J S, M D, store and res 731 Asbury ave.
Walton B F, West ave bel Fourteenth st, also Camden, N J.
Warner F B, carpenter, 1428 Asbury ave.

G. E. Palen Ph. B. M. D

DR. PALEN'S COTTAGE.

DR. PALEN'S COTTAGES ON THE OCEAN FRONT.

Watson C H, grader, West ave abv Fifth st.
Wert C M, store and res 713 Asbury ave.
Whitaker W C, 1230 Asbury ave, also Bridgeton, N J.
Whiteside F R, 1236 Asbury ave, also Phila, Pa.
Willets J S Capt, N cor Seventh st and Central ave.
Williams T P, Asbury ave abv First st.
Williams C J, 423 Wesley ave, also Phila, Pa.
Willets S Mrs, West ave abv Seventh st.
Wilcox J N Mrs, 842 Central ave, also Phila, Pa.
Willoughby W, West ave abv First st, also Phila, Pa.
Wood H M Miss, E cor Asbury ave and West st, also Phila, Pa.
Wolf J, coal, res "Sea Breeze," 704 Central ave.

Z

Zeigler E, 717 Central ave, also Phila, Pa.
Zane W S Rev, 1208 Asbury ave, also N J Conf.

There are a large number of houses the names of whose occu-
pants do not appear. These cottages are occupied by different
tenants every year, perhaps by several in a season. This fact pre-
cludes the possibility of securing a very large percentage of our
summer residents.

Guide Book and Directory.

"Who can alight on as happy a shore,
All the world o'er, all the world o'er,
Whither away? Listen and stay."

The island upon which Ocean City is built, is located on the
New Jersey coast, ten miles south of Atlantic City. It contains an
area of over three and one-half square miles, or about 2000 acres,
and stretches between Great Egg Harbor Bay and Thoroughfare
Sound on one side, and the Atlantic Ocean on the other side for
seven miles, thus having the peculiar advantage of an entire length
of ocean frontage. The northern and southern limits are bounded
by Great Egg Harbor Inlet and Corson's Inlet. The strand of
firmly-packed sand 200 feet wide is higher than any point along
the New Jersey coast. It slopes gently to the sea, and is smooth
and as hard as a floor, without any quicksands or treacherous
grounds. When the storms of the equinox sweep the seaboard,
Great Egg Harbor Bar is an invaluable protection to the city; this,
even if it were possible to create by mechanical skill, would cost
fabulous sums of money. At all times, the waves breaking upon
it lose their force before rolling up on the strand.

The island is a chosen spot of nature. The soil possesses
peculiar properties, and protected by the sheltering sand hills which
skirt the shore, is productive of a most luxuriant flora, blending
the growth of the tropics with that of the temperate regions.
Responding to this wondrous creative influence, it stands out from
the dreary stretch of dull marsh lands and white sands of the coast
fair and green. In clearing the land of its dense vegetable growth,
many of the cedars have been left. While this tree cannot com-

JESSE CONVER,
City Councilman.

DR. J. E. WAGGONER,
Oldest Resident Physician of Ocean City.

H. G. STEELMAN,
City Treasurer.

pare in beauty with others of the order *coniferæ*, the stately fir, or the graceful larch, yet as it stands with roots firmly grasping soil almost swept by the waves, its gnarled and straggling branches grappling with the fierce Atlantic storms, reminding us of the rugged strength which characterizes the tree of its family from which Solomon hewed the timbers for the building of the temple at Jerusalem—the cedars of Lebanon—it forms a pleasing back-ground for the mottled ash bark, shining leaves and scarlet fruit of the hollies, the pale green of the willows, and the crimson and gold of the autumn maples. A thousand varieties of wild flowers mingle their delicate bloom in the thickets of grape vines, clematis, bayberry and alder bushes. The floral gem of our northern forests, trailing arbutus, flourishes about the roots of the southern magnolia ; the dull purple of the cinquefoil, usually found in cold bogs, mingles with the yellow blossoms of the prickly cactus, while among the lush grasses of the meadows grow hundreds of varieties of marsh and aquatic herbs, which in their season star the earth with a rich profusion of variety and color.

From early spring till autumn the air is redolent with the odor of flowers. Song birds, the whistling cardinal of brilliant plumage, the yellow oriole, the meadow lark, thrush, robin, and song sparrow build their nests among the branches of the low trees, and in the thickets of the eglantine and beach grass. The place has been well known to sportsmen. Immense numbers of wild fowl found cover in the thick underbrush about the inland ponds, and the abundant growth of small fruits afforded them sustenance. In the spring and autumn wild geese, ducks and other migratory birds, while passing north or south, rested here in their long flight and regaled themselves, the discordant notes of one flock scarcely dying away before a dark line, wedge or cloud in the distance denoted the approach of another one. The stately blue heron, now seldom seen, stalked majestically over the meadows or stood upon the margin of the pools in profound meditation. The tall white "booby" covered acres of ground midway of the island with nests, from which were gathered eggs by people living on the mainland. The loon uttered,

2

its mournful note as it winged its slow flight inland or folded its
lengthy legs and wings in an apparently inextricable mass in
alighting. Curlew, plover, and infinite varieties of snipe, waded out
after the receding wave in quest of unwary mussels, their low cries
mingling with the angry scream of the bald eagle, as he darted
into the waters for his prey, or oftener robbed the hard-working
fish hawk. Twenty-seven varieties of sea gulls visit the coast.
They are divided into two general classes: summer gulls and
winter gulls. They vary in size from a pigeon to a goose. The
winter gulls are the largest, and come in November; in May
they return to Labrador.

On this part of the coast is found a wonderful variety of forms
of ocean life, from the low, shapeless mollusk to the gigantic
cetacean. This fact is apparent in the choice of the location of
the Biological Society buildings of the University of Pennsylvania,
ten miles to the south, at Sea Isle City. To see the ocean when it
is terrible in its beauty, one must visit it during the fall or winter
months. It is then, when lashed into fury by the winds, that the
depths are stirred and its treasures thrown up on the beach. The
strand looks at times as though a polar had swept over it and
left a thousand fantastic forms of ice, so clear that when the sun's
rays strike them they radiate every color of the rainbow. These
are jelly fish, dead and divested of their digestive organs, thus
making the illusion more complete, as that is the only part of their
bodies not transparent. Coustellations of star fish, the quaint tiny
sea horse, "sailor's razors" and "pincushions," the graceful "sea
robin," conchs, clams and sea snails may be seen in abundance.

On the eighth of October a finback or rorqual whale washed
ashore measuring sixty-eight feet. The tail measured fifteen feet
across the flukes, and if Neptune had harnessed it to his chariot,
he would have required a bit thirteen feet long to have controlled
his charger. It was a monster of its kind, and the skeleton is the
largest owned by any museum in the world.

Lying near the 39th degree of latitude, the climate is that of
Annapolis, Maryland. Spring comes early. Summer is rendered
delightful by the cool sea breezes. Autumn, with its gorgeous

F. P. CANFIELD,
City Councilman

"The Illinois," Mrs. H. D. Canfield, Proprietress.

coloring, dreamy haze and bright skies, lingers long. The close proximity of the gulf stream adds greatly to the salutary influence of the climate. The winters are tempered by its warm current, thus making an all-the-year-round residence in every way desirable. Invalids are loud in their praises of its benefits. What better inspiration can be wished for than the music of the pines, the roar of the ocean, the invigorating blast of the Atlantic north wind? This is a part of our birthright, from which we cannot afford to be kept out.

The island was formerly known as Peck's Beach. There may be found still further back, in the archives of the Courts of London, a document in which it was known as Pete's Beach. It has little written history save that of its location and wrecks. Of a period when a race computing time by nights and moons built their mud lodges along the shore, no record is given. Tradition only hands its history down to us interwoven with the beautiful legends of the peaceful tribes of Delawares or Lenni-Lenapes. If we measure time by the years since the island has been inhabited, it is but a short step back from this bright scene of civilization to the time when their swift pirogues shot out from the shore filled with dusky braves, gorgeous in paint and feathers, and with squaws of beautiful form clothed in rudely-made garments fringed with the hair of the red deer, still found in Southern New Jersey, while wampum made from the clam shells of the beach adorned their black unbound hair. Pirates have anchored here without fear of molestation, and borne from the hold of the vessel treasures of gold, jewels and rich merchandise to bury beneath these sands. Their implements of warfare have been dug up but recently, quite near. One of these, a long, pointed iron rod; half-way of its length was fastened a knife fashioned like a hand sickle. The evident intention of its use was first to draw the victim toward the executioner with the knife, and then impale him on the rod.

The first topographical survey of the island was made to Thomas Budd, October 7, 1695. In 1750, about 500 acres of land located between Ninth street and the north point of the beach, were bought of him by John Somers, Lord Chancellor of England,

and cousin of John Lord, Right Honorable Earl of Hardwick. This tract of land remained in the possession of the Somers family for one hundred and thirty years. The first houses upon the island known to be built by white people, were located, one near the north point of beach, occupied by Hanna Kittle, the other in the neighborhood of Ninth street and Asbury avenue, occupied by John Robinson. Thirty-three years ago Parker Miller, and Louisa, his wife, with four little children, braved the solitude and erected a home. For over twenty years they were the only residents. Their intercourse with the outside world was when sportsmen came gunning for wild fowl, when a vessel was cast away, or "beach parties" came across the bay for a day's recreation. Mr. Miller was engaged in raising cattle, planting oysters, and watching the coast for wrecks. He has acquired by his long residence and direct observation, a better knowledge of the island from its primeval condition to its present high state of development, than any one living.

FIRST M. E. CHURCH.

REV. W. A. MASSEY,
Pastor of First M. E. Church.

Great Egg Harbor Bay.

This picturesque, landlocked sheet of water, teeming with blue-fish, sheepshead, oysters, and shellfish of every description, received its name from the large numbers of gulls' eggs found in the surrounding meadows. The gentle ebb and flow of the tide, submerging and revealing the emerald beauty of its tiny green islands, the white-winged sea craft passing rapidly to and fro or resting lazily on the blue waters, the throbbing steamers with their long wakes of white foam, form an endless panorama, from which the weary toiler, the dispirited pleasure seeker, nor the invalid, can ever grow weary. Away to the southwest, Thoroughfare Sound sweeps out through the meadows, till it is lost to view in the shadow of the pines. Following the line of the bay, now curving to the west, Beasley's Point is plainly visible. During Revolutionary times, a watch was kept at this place from a "crows-nest" or lookout, and if any British vessels were seen, a bell was rung and the inhabitants of the surrounding country quickly gathered at the Point to repulse the soldiers should they come in on a foraging expedition, as was frequently done. At one time all the men of the village were absent, and a young woman, Rachel Stillwell, was keeping watch ; she espied a British man-o'-war lying just outside of the inlet. Quickly dropping the spy-glass she gave the alarm, but before it was responded to the British had lowered their row boats and were speeding across the bay. Summoning the women of the hamlet, a cannon was quickly rolled into posi-tion, and with her own hands she applied a brand to the touch-hole, and quickly reloading, sent peal after peal across the waters, completely routing the redcoats.

Sweeping down past Beasley's Point, the waters of the Tucka-hoe, Middle, and Great Egg Harbor rivers empty into the bay. In the dim perspective, masts and sails are outlined against the sky; in nearer view, schooners laden with wood, oysters, and freight of various kinds, are hurrying out to the ocean, bound for different points all along the coast.

Historic Somers' Point next marks the curve of the shore. From its wharves have sailed out brave soldiers of the Revolution and daring and skillful navigators. Many of these who have "gone down to the sea in ships" have left behind them wives, sweethearts and mothers, who differed only from the heroines of fiction in that the tragedy and pathos of their lives were real, for as they left the port, they sailed out of the lives of those standing on shore, and all that ever floated back was a rumor, perhaps, of a fragment of wreck cast up on some distant coast, bearing the name or some trace of the vessel.

Still following the line of the shore, now lost to view, and now clear and distinct, Longport may be seen. Its prominent wharf is visible for many miles out at sea. This point of land forms the last boundary of the bay, and is divided from Ocean City by Great Egg Harbor Inlet. On its opposite side it is washed for miles by the Atlantic Ocean. The same character of the beach as that of Ocean City is noticeable. Longport was founded by M. Simpson McCullough in 1882. Palatial houses and tasteful and convenient cottages adorn its streets and avenues. The Aberdeen Hotel, conducted by W. Lamborn and Mrs. Elizabeth Kitts, is one of the finest on the coast. The sanitary arrangements are complete in every detail. The facilities for bathing, boating and fishing are nowhere excelled, and Longport promises to be in the near future the Newport of Southern New Jersey.

At the wharves at Ocean City yachts are constantly in readiness to take parties out fishing or sailing on the bay or ocean. The Atlantic Coast Steamboat Company operates a line of steamboats between Ocean City, Longport and Somers' Point. A large steamer is run to the fishing banks in the ocean daily during the summer. This is provided with lines, bait, and everything necessary for the comfort and enjoyment of its patrons. This is patronized by invalids and pleasure seekers, aside from those who go for the sake of fishing. While enjoying the refreshing sea air, they can rest in the cabins or beneath canopies, shaded from the sun.

R. FISHER'S RESIDENCE.

R. Fisher's Office Buildings and Twin Cottages.

The Founders of Ocean City.

The name of Ocean City will ever be associated with that of the Lakes—Hon. Simon Lake and his three sons, Ezra B., S. Wesley and James E., all born and reared in Southern New Jersey. Early in life the sons were led to enter the Christian ministry, and became members of the New Jersey M. E. Conference, and have since filled honorable positions. After some years, the attention of Rev. E. B. Lake was directed towards the establishing of a seaside resort, where the sale of alcoholic liquors should be prohibited and the sanctity of the Sabbath preserved. The tract of land, Peck's Beach, presented itself to his mind as the one to be redeemed for the purpose. Mr. Lake was eminently fitted for the work and entered upon it with an enthusiasm which is ever fresh and constant. Hon. Simon Lake, recognizing the possibilities of the enterprise, immediately engaged with him, and the admirable plan of the City and its acquired facilities are largely due to his far-seeing wisdom and sound executive ability. Revs. S. Wesley and James E. next came forward, and have, since that time, labored with Rev. E. B. Lake in the interests of the City.

Shortly after the enterprise was fairly under way, Hon. Simon Lake was stricken with a sudden and fatal illness, and passed away November 28, 1881. He was looked to as a leader in the affairs of church and state by all with whom he was associated. He carried his 68 years as sturdily as any other man of 40. Tall and broad of frame, strong in arm and voice, he reached the close of his earthly career with faculties of mind and body unimpaired by time or disease. His untimely death was mourned throughout the country.

Ocean City Association.

OFFICERS AND MANAGERS.

President, Rev. W. B. Wood; Vice-President, Rev. W. H. Burrell; Secretary, Hon. S. Lake; Treasurer, C. Matthews, Esq.; Superintendent, Rev. E. B. Lake; Rev. W. E. Boyle, Rev. S. W. Lake, C. Matthews, Jr., and Rev. J. E. Lake.

Through the efforts of the Lake family a company was formed with the above name and members. Active operations toward bringing forth a city from beneath the sand hills and out of the thickets commenced October 20, 1879, by securing the land and issuing stock. The first topographical survey was made by William Lake during the fall and winter following. The part known as section A was staked off into avenues, streets and lots. This was quickly cleared of brushwood and timber; thousands of feet of ditching were dug for drainage, and hundreds of loads of brushwood were placed at the north point of beach for the purpose of gathering the moving sand and extending the ocean front. Lots to the value of $85,000 were disposed of, and another portion of land, known as section B, surveyed and laid out. A wharf, 125 feet long by 72 feet wide, was built at an enormous cost. This was connected with the City by a good road over the meadows, 1000 feet long, and a board walk running parallel with it the entire distance. Dwelling houses, unpretentious at first, commenced to spring up. These were soon succeeded by large and commodious buildings. The first building erected was the little Pioneer Cottage, then standing on the rear of the lot now occupied by the Association Office. It was used as a boarding house for the mechanics at work on the Island, and was sometimes occupied by forty men. The first hotel, the Ocean House, was built by I. B. Smith;

R. C. ROBINSON,
Editor and Proprietor of the Ocean City Sentinel.

now the far-famed "Brighton," owned and conducted by R. R. Sooy. A newspaper was issued May, 1880. A railroad was built from Pleasantville to Somers' Point, known as the Pleasantville and Ocean City Railroad. This was formally opened October 26, 1880. A steamboat was purchased to ply between Somers' Point and Ocean City, thus completing connection with the outside world. A Turnpike Company was organized to build a road from Beesley's Point to Ocean City, which, together with a bridge over Thorough-fare Sound, was completed the following spring. A local church was organized and a camp meeting held for ten days.

This brief summary of a little more than a year's work is but one page in the rapid advancement of the City. The development during so short a period necessarily had the effect of stimulating and bringing forward new purchasers and residents, and the tide of progress has never abated. The success of an enterprise of this kind is not brought about without formidable difficulties. The toil and anxiety are best known to those who have participated in a work of its kind. The Association has tenaciously adhered to the principles first laid down, and sympathetic and fraternal relations now exist where the lava tide of dissension and strife threatened disaster.

Its present officers and managers are :

President, Rev. J. B. Graw, D. D.
Vice-President, Rev. W. B. Wood, D. D.
Secretary, Rev. S. Wesley Lake.
Treasurer, Dr. G. E. Palen.
Superintendent, Rev. E. B. Lake.
George L. Horn, G. B. Langley, H. B. Howell, Rev. James E. Lake.

Ocean City.

Ocean City was created by an act of incorporation April 30, 1884. The first council consisted of G. P. Moore, Mayor; Parker Miller, Rev. W. H. Burrell, Correll Doughty and Enoch Green. The administration of the two mayors and the councilmen who have served with them since then, has been attended with stability and prosperity. This is shown in the steady throbbing pulsation which marks the life and business interests of a city which is under no bond of debt, and has never realized the paralyzing effects of a sudden boom, whose growth has been steadily upward from the first. When the government was vested in a mayor and council, the original design of the City was carried out, but upon a broad and liberal basis. The avenues through which vice and immorality enter are guarded only to such an extent as to be a protection to liberty and pleasure, which are in no way restrained, and Ocean City has a genuine air of respectability and refinement.

To follow, step by step, its growth and progress is impossible, but not twelve years have elapsed, and a city of beautiful homes stretches from bay to ocean and for miles up and down the island. Spacious and elegant summer residences of prominent citizens of Philadelphia, Camden, New York, and inland cities north and south, adorn its wide streets and avenues. Accommodations for the entertainment of guests are nowhere excelled. The hotels are thoroughly equipped; boarding cottages, large and small, may be found to suit every taste. There are miles of graveled streets and sidewalks, boardwalks on the strand, public schools, stores of every description, steamboat and railroad facilities, excellent telegraphic and mail services, and everything which may be found in cities much older. The Auditorium, occupying the center of the camp

JOHN R. KENDRICK.

"SIESTA" Jno. R. KENDRICK. 820 Wesley Ave.

ground, is a handsome structure, with a seating capacity of two thousand. The public school is a well-built, prominent edifice, and is supplied with a most efficient corps of teachers. The Excursion House on the strand adds greatly to the convenience of visitors. Bath houses, restaurants, carousels, and booths of every description, spring up at every point.

The M. E. church was dedicated August, 1891. Rev. W. A. Massey, the pastor, is not only an able preacher, but an indefatigable worker as well. During his pastorate the membership has been greatly increased, and through the quiet months of winter, as well as the exciting summer season, the church is always well filled. In a short time a new parsonage adjoining the church will be completed.

Ocean City has the additional attraction for moral people that the liquor traffic is prohibited. A clause in all deeds calls for the forfeiture of title if the vice is allowed to flourish on the premises.

Rents are very reasonable, either for the season or by the year. Cottages, furnished or unfurnished, can be rented from fifty dollars upwards. The surrounding country, through its rich soil, furnishes the best of vegetables, fruits, etc., in great abundance. These are brought direct to the City by the farmers and truckers themselves, and wholesaled to the markets or retailed from the wagons to customers.

Several routes are available by which the City may be reached from the imperial eastern cities—New York and Philadelphia. These are within a few hours by rail, and the important cities up and down the coast are brought into close touch either by rail or water.

Ocean City has officials and citizens of whom it may be justly proud. Besides those of whom sketches are given are J. T. Adams, proprietor of the Traymore and owner of the Lafayette; R. R. Sooy, the genial host of the Brighton; N. Corson, one of the first builders of the City, a man whose life is marked by sterling integrity; Capt. Isaac Lee, spending his declining years in peaceful, contented retirement; 'Squire Myers, progressive and enterprising; Dr. D. W. Bartine, professor of mathematics in the public schools

of Philadelphia; Joseph Brower, a retired merchant of Philadelphia;
W. Godfrey, one of the earliest pioneers of Ocean City; Assessor
R. Ludlam; R. Fisher, whose extensive business speaks for itself;
J. T. Price, the enterprising host of the Ocean City House; S.
Schurch, of the Bellevue; F. Schmitt, a self-made, and for many
years a prominent business man of Philadelphia, and Hiram Steelman, grocer. Among our younger men who owe their success
largely to their own efforts since they came to Ocean City, are City
Treasurer H. G. Steelman, owner and proprietor of the largest
grocery store in the City; City Clerk and Real Estate Agent H. B.
Adams; Abel D. Scull, architect and builder, whose work is among
the finest in the City; John Gandy, grocer; the Sampson Brothers,
contractors; R. B. Stites, lumber dealer; Stonehill & Adams,
stone-masons. The younger members of the city council, F. P.
Canfield and J. Steelman, are coming rapidly to the front as business men, and are showing themselves to be men capable of being
vested with municipal powers.

Among our noted summer residents are M. C. Clelland, of the
Ridge Avenue Railway; E. Brucker, a retired merchant of Philadelphia; the Davis brothers, of Camden; H. Gerlach, a prominent
jeweler of Philadelphia; C. H. Schermerhorn, secretary and treasurer of the Niagara Mining and Smelting Company of Utah; Dr.
C. E. Edwards, of Haddonfield, N. J.; F. R. Whitesides, of the firm
Rush Whitesides & Sons, Philadelphia; Godfrey Krouse, a prominent Philadelphia plumber; Rev. W. Huckle, of New York; Dr.
F. R. Graham, a prominent physician of Chester, Pa., and a host of
others whom we hope to mention more fully in a future edition of
the Guide Book and Directory.

LIFE-SAVING STATION "OCEAN CITY."

THE AUDITORIUM.

Biographical Sketches.

MAYOR G. P. MOORE.

Mr. Moore was born in Chester county, Pa., of Quaker parents. He received the education of the common schools of the day, and afterwards learned the trade of a carpenter. In 1854 he removed to Michigan and engaged in farming, but returned to his native state four years later and went into business as a builder. He was twice a volunteer in the late Rebellion ; failing to pass the physical examination the first time, he was the second time accepted. Mr. Moore also holds the position of a notary public, is a prominent member of the society of Odd Fellows, and a director of the Cape May County Agricultural Association. He has held many positions of private trust, not one of which has ever been violated.

Mr. Moore is possessed of strong religious tendencies. The churches of Ceresco Circuit, Michigan, were founded through his missionary labors. At the battle of Bull Run he was commissioned by the Christian Commission to go to the front to care for the wounded and dying. One instance alone of how his life in this direction is respected, is shown by the fact that when called by the United States Court to Baltimore to give testimony in a great life insurance trial, he was honored by the court suspending business to allow him to transact some private business with them in time to return home without traveling on the Sabbath. He came to Ocean City in 1881, and has held the office of mayor since its incorporation, with the exception of one term. He is a progressive official, honored by all parties, and has served the city well.

EX-MAYOR J. E. PRYOR, M.D.

Dr. Pryor is descended from a family prominent in the state of Indiana for over 160 years; noted through Colonial and Revolutionary times for the men it furnished both as officers and privates to the patriot armies engaged in warfare on the western frontier, when the Indians, led on by their great chief Tecumseh, constituted such a terrible foe.

Dr. Pryor was born in the Wabash Valley, at the old "Pryor Homestead," almost in sight of the battle ground of Tippecanoe. He received his preliminary education at the common schools, and when eighteen years of age commenced teaching in this department. During this period his spare time was devoted to the prosecution of his own studies. In the spring of 1885, he entered the Detroit Medical College, from which institution he was graduated three years later; he also received a course of instruction at the Philadelphia Polyclinic. He came to Ocean City in 1888, and soon acquired a successful practice. The duties which devolved upon him in this capacity were discharged in a thorough and conscientious manner. Dr. Pryor has displayed through his career the perseverance and courage which will continue to bring to him in the future as it has in the past the success which is ever the result of these attributes.

DR. GILBERT E. PALEN.

Dr. G. E. Palen has been one of the regular summer residents of Ocean City since 1881. He has shown his faith in its future by investing largely in lots, and building several cottages. He is deeply interested in retaining the temperance and religious principles upon which the place was founded, and thus keeping Ocean City free from the vices which so predominate in most resorts of this kind. He is one of the stockholders of Ocean City Association, and has been its treasurer for a number of years.

Dr. Palen was born in Palenville, N. Y., May 3, 1832. His father, Rufus Palen, was of Quaker stock, and was a well-known

WILLIAM LAKE.

tanner and leather dealer, being a partner of Shepherd Knapp, and a member of the firms of Knapp & Palen, Palen & Flagler, etc. After preparing himself for college, Dr. Palen first obtained a thorough knowledge of the tanning business at the Fallsburgh, N. Y., tannery, in which his father's estate had a large interest. Then entering Brown University, he went with several of the professors and a number of students to Yale, where he graduated with the degree of Ph.B. in the "famous class" of 1853. He then pursued a medical course at the New York University, which he subsequently completed at the Albany Medical College, graduating from the latter in 1855 as a doctor of medicine.

But it having been the wish of his father that his eldest son should follow his business, Dr. Palen, in 1856, entered into partnership with his uncle by marriage, George W. Northrop, and built an oak tannery at Canadensis, Pa., afterward taking one of his brothers in as a partner, under the firm name of Palen & Northrop. Afterwards, with his two brothers, Dr. Palen built another tannery at Tunkhannock, Pa., but the business proving unprofitable for the manufacturer, owing to the unequal distribution of the profits between himself and the dealers, the doctor determined to retire. The building of tanneries in the woods, cutting down trees, etc., is genuine pioneer work, and to this the doctor was peculiarly fitted by his active temperament. In 1860 the doctor married Elizabeth Gould, daughter of John B. Gould, of Roxbury, N. Y. He became a member of the M. E. church at Canadensis, and at this period his career as a Prohibitionist and temperance worker begins, voting the Prohibition ticket, the voters being so few that he was obliged to write his own. Removing afterwards to Tunkhannock, Pa., he engaged actively in the struggle for local option, which, finally gained, was lost by the treachery or half-heartedness of some of its supporters.

In 1876, after a careful examination of the compound oxygen process, he entered into partnership with Dr. Starkey, under the firm name of Starkey & Palen, the former bringing into the concern his perfected system, and Dr. Palen the business experience and requisite capital. From this time the business has prospered wonderfully, and the treatment is now known throughout the world. The doctor is an active and honored member of the M. E. Board of Church Extension, and president of the Niagara Mining and Smelting Co., and is always active in every movement for the public good. He has been several times candidate for mayor and recorder of Philadelphia on the Prohibition ticket, accepting each time his anticipated defeat with resignation, but never for a moment despairing of the final triumph of Prohibition.

J. S. WAGGONER, M.D.

Dr. Waggoner was born in Perry county, Pa., where he resided during his boyhood. He afterward removed to Carlisle, Pa., and engaged in the study of medicine. In 1860 he was graduated from the University of Pennsylvania. At the outbreaking of the Rebellion, he was appointed assistant surgeon of the 5th Pennsylvania Cavalry (Cameron Dragoons), and was also physician to the Eastern Insane Asylum of Virginia at Williamsburg. He was mustered out as a supernumerary of the 5th Pennsylvania Cavalry, and immediately appointed assistant surgeon to the 84th Pennsylvania Infantry, from which position he was shortly afterward appointed to that of surgeon. In 1864 he resigned, and was appointed post surgeon of the United States General Hospital at Beverly. Here he acquired an enviable reputation as a surgeon. At the battle of Chancellorsville he was carried from the field wounded and given up for dead, but was resuscitated and cared for by S. S. Fowler, now of North Carolina.

After the war he was engaged in private practice in New Jersey. He came to Ocean City when it was first started, and established the pioneer drug store, still continuing the practice of medicine. He has served as borough clerk and city councilman.

Dr. Waggoner is thoroughly conscientious in all his work. The positions which he has held, and the offices he has filled, have been honored by the manner in which he has discharged the duties of each. A retiring disposition has prevented a greater advancement, which his ability has rendered possible.

H. E. ADAMS,
City Clerk.

W. LAKE, C. E.

Mr. Lake was born at Bargaintown, N. J., April 27, 1838. His boyhood was spent with his father, working at the blacksmith trade. Not satisfied with the educational advantages of the day, he entered upon a course of studies by himself and was soon teaching in the public schools. At a very early age he received an appointment as civil engineer, and his progress since then has been steadily upward. He was elected to numerous township offices, and was, in 1863, appointed commissioner of deeds. In 1875 he was appointed master in chancery, and the same year elected to the office of justice of the peace of Atlantic county, which position he held until his removal to Ocean City. His work commenced in this City with the earliest movement made towards its development. He has surveyed every foot of the island and examined every original title from 1690 down to the time it was purchased by the Ocean City Association, and has drawn over nineteen hundred deeds. Mr. Lake is in consequence very closely identified with the progress and growth of the City, and has in his possession much interesting and important data concerning its history. He is at present engaged in preparing a brief of title of a tract of six thousand acres in Atlantic county, for the purpose of forming a new settlement.

JESSE CONVER.

City Councilman Conver, now holding the office for the third term, is a native of Pennsylvania, born in Montgomery county, March 29, 1834. He engaged in the tin and sheet-iron business at twenty years of age, and shortly afterwards removed to Philadelphia, where he carried on roofing, heating and range business very extensively. He came to Ocean City in 1881, and has since engaged in the same business. Mr. Conver is one of the few men who, when coming in contact with the business world, do not allow its influence to draw them from their own conscientiousness of truth. and right, who maintain a strict integrity in all their business transactions. The influence of his early life among the hills of Pennsylvania, of simple habits and firmly ingrained principles of right, are still exerted, and may be felt and seen in his daily life.

3

R. H. THORN.

Mr. Thorn is a Pennsylvanian, born and reared in Frankford, Philadelphia. He received his education in the public schools, and afterwards learned the carpenter's trade. He came to Ocean City May 4, 1885, and having a previous knowledge of the business, purchased stock and opened a hardware and house-furnishing store at his present stand, 801 Asbury avenue. Mr. Thorn is a brilliant example of what grit, determination and close application to business will do. Coming at a time when everything was new, the permanent population small, the situation was not a promising one. In 1887 he purchased two lots adjoining the stand he occupied and built store No. 805 Asbury avenue. In 1890 he bought the stand where he commenced business, and in 1891 built still another store between 801 and 805, together with a dwelling house facing on Eighth street. Mr. Thorn has now the largest establishment of its kind in the City, with a constantly increasing business. He has served as city councilman, and has held other positions of trust, both public and private.

R. C. ROBINSON.

One of our rising young men is Postmaster R. C. Robinson, editor and proprietor of the *Ocean City Sentinel*. Mr. Robinson was born in Atlantic county, N. J., in 1862. His father died when he was nine years of age, and he was early thrown on his own resources. At sixteen years of age he entered a wholesale dry-goods house, but finding the business distasteful, he engaged to learn the printing business in the *Banner* office at Beverly, N. J. He then accepted a position with A. L. English, of the *Atlantic Review*, Atlantic City. Mr. Robinson was first in the employ and was then associated with Mr. English in business for over six years. During this time he was editor and manager of the *May's Landing Record*, and assistant editor of the Philadelphia journal, *Over the Mountains and Down by the Sea*. He came to Ocean City in 1885, and forming a partnership with W. H. Fenton, purchased the *Ocean*

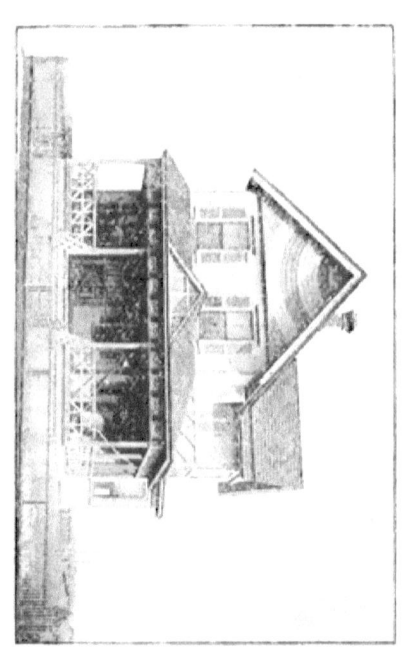

C. H. SCHERMERHORN'S COTTAGE.

City Sentinel, and in a short time became sole proprietor. In 1888 he represented Ocean City in the board of freeholders of Cape May county. He was appointed postmaster in 1889. Upon assuming the duties of this position, he immediately set about having the mail service extended and the office designated a money order office, succeeding in both. Mr. Robinson is possessed of those faculties which constitute the elements of success—hard labor and strict attention to whatever line of business in which he may be engaged.

JOHN RYLAND KENDRICK.

Touching at Ocean City in 1884, Mr. and Mrs. J. R. Kendrick, of Philadelphia, were quickly impressed with its beauty and desirability as a summer resort. In 1889 they built a tasteful " Queen Anne " cottage on Wesley avenue, below Eighth street, facing the ocean, and possessing in its location every essential of an ideal seaside home. Mr. Kendrick descends from a New England family long prominent in clerical, educational and business circles. His grandfather, the Rev. Clark Kendrick, was an early Baptist chaplain of the Vermont legislature. Prof. A. C. Kendrick, D.D., LL.D., founder of the "University of Rochester" and a member of the board which produced the present revised version of the Scriptures; also the late Rev. J. Ryland Kendrick, D.D., an eloquent preacher and teacher, and president of Vassar College, are uncles of the gentleman whose career we note. The New England Kendricks are in line direct from Edward Kendrick, an eminent merchant of London and Rotterdam, and Lord Mayor of London in the time of " Bloody Mary." This ancestor married Susannah Cranmer, a niece of Archbishop Cranmer, whom the Papists burned at the stake. " Virtue is honor" is the family motto. J. R. Kendrick, whose face appears elsewhere, is in his forty-third year, and conducts a publishing business at 1001 Chestnut street, Philadelphia. He also owns and edits "The American Carpet and Upholstery Trade," a journal of wide influence in its sphere, founded by him in 1883. Mr. Kendrick gives much attention to the manufacture of textiles, and has several times served the United States government in the collation of industrial statistics. He served in the tenth and eleventh United States censuses, also as special treasury officer under Secretaries Sherman and Windom. He loves the "quill," and has done some writing of permanent value. His articles on "Carpets and Upholstery" for Appleton's Cyclopædia are considered authentic data, and his report on the "Carpet Industry of Pennsylvania," made to Governor Beaver's administration, was an exhaustive and laborious piece of work. This appears in the report for 1889, Bureau of Internal Affairs. Mr. Kendrick is devoted to his family, which consists of his amiable wife, two sons and two daughters. The family entertain liberally at their summer home and possess a wide circle of friends.

RESIDENCE OF J. P. HAND,
Contractor and Builder, 721 Central Avenue.

Life-Saving Service.

The complications of the system of the Life-Saving Service are comparatively little known to those living inland. This was imperfectly carried on for some years previous to 1872, but since that time means are taken every year for its greater perfection, and as it reaches its strong arms out to aid mariners in distress and to preserve property from destruction, the magnitude of its importance can only be estimated by the long marine official records of its work. The Atlantic coast is patrolled from Maine to Florida, the Gulf of Mexico and the great lakes their entire coast. Stations are placed at suitable distances apart, furnished with all the necessary appliances for the work. From September 1st to May 1st they are occupied by seven life-guards, one extra going on December 1st. The other four months of the year, the season when few severe storms occur, the captain alone remains; and as a large percentage of those living on the coast are sailors or fishermen, a volunteer crew can be easily secured should it be necessary. The uniform consists of a navy blue Guernsey, embroidered across the breast with the scarlet letters L. S. S., and the name of the station to which they belong; navy blue pantaloons, overcoat and cap. Around the latter is fastened a ribbon in which is woven in gilt letters the words U. S. Life-Saving Service. Another cap, worn in cold or stormy weather, is a woolen skull cap, called the "Normandy Fisherman."

The men as a class are stalwart, well built, and present a fine appearance. Watches are kept as on board ship, four hours long. Every night at sunset two guards are sent from each station, one going north and one south. Each one is met at a given point by a guard from the station on either side, with whom they exchange

checks.   When this kind of communication is impossible, on
account of a bay or an inlet coming between two stations, a clock
is placed at the end of the beat in a wooden post, bored out in the
side large enough to receive it, where it is secured by an iron plate;
this registers every visit made by a guard.   At eight o'clock these
guards return, and two others take their place, who exchange
checks or register, as do also those of the succeeding watches.
Each guard is supplied with rockets with which to warn vessels
that are approaching too near the shore and to answer signals of
distress.   A lookout is kept from sunrise to sunset, and every passing vessel noted down.   A journal is kept of each day's proceed-
ings, which is forwarded to Washington.   On cloudy or stormy
days the coast is patrolled during the day as well as night.

ROUTINE OF DUTY.

The guards are required to keep in constant practice.   Tuesday
of each week they go out in the life-boat.   This, by a simple yet
very ingenious contrivance will bail itself out should it become
filled with water.   Wednesday is flag day.   A few of the most
important of a code of fourteen thousand signals are practiced.
By this means conversation can be carried on with ships far out at
sea.   Thursday they practice with the breeches buoy; this is oper-
ated in the following manner: A line is shot from a mortar out to
the sinking ship.   To the end of this line is fastened a whip-line,
and to this a hawser.   A wooden tag is fastened to the hawser with
directions printed on it, one side in French and the other side in
English, for making it fast and how to assist in working the buoy.
As soon as it is made fast, the guards send the buoy out to the
ship; this is a skillfully contrived basket in the shape of a huge
pair of breeches.   A passenger steps into them, swings out over
the angry waters and is hauled quickly to shore, the buoy return-
ing to the ship in an incredibly short space of time.   This is used
only when it is impossible to reach the vessel in a boat.   Friday

R. H. THORN'S STORES AND RESIDENCE.

the performance of resuscitating the drowned is gone through with. Saturday is general cleaning day.

Too much praise cannot be lavished on these brave men, who in times of extreme peril never falter. No means, however daring, are left untried for the rescue of life. The keepers of the three stations at Ocean City were all seafaring men years before entering the L. S. S. In their travels they have visited many strange countries. The valuable and interesting information given by them, the courtesy which ever marks the deportment of a life-guard, render the visits of our guests to the Life-Saving stations delightfully entertaining.

Wrecks.

Peck's Beach has a distinct history written in its driftwood. The features of the coast are constantly changing, as the sea encroaches upon one place and recedes from another. Great Egg Harbor Bar is dangerous to mariners with large craft, on account of its continually shifting sands, and requires the special attention of the coast surveyors. A chart of one year varies greatly from that of another. Its treacherous character is plainly shown in the vast number of wrecks which have strewn the beach. Imagination and fancy have not the monopoly of romance and tragedy. Truth here claims a share beyond the power of either. Since the Life Saving Service has been in operation, and insurance companies have grown more watchful, the number is greatly diminished. In the following pages we give a few of the most interesting.

THE FAME.

The first of which we can gain an authentic account is that of the brig Fame. This vessel was sent out with a number of others to protect the inhabitants of Cape May county from the incursions of the British and refugees. She was in command of Captain William Treen, of Egg Harbor, and made a number of captures of vessels much larger than herself. The night of February 22, 1781, while lying at the anchoring point in Great Egg Harbor Bay rejoicing over a victory just achieved, she was capsized in a heavy gale, with twenty-eight of a crew of thirty-two men on board. Four attempted to swim ashore; three succeeded in landing at the north point of Peck's Beach, the fourth one drowned. Help reached the vessel at daylight, but of twenty-four brave men who had faced shot and shell, tempest and flood, twenty had succumbed to the sleep of death from exposure to the intense cold; the four remaining ones kept alive by walking rapidly and constantly up and down the side of the capsized vessel.

ABEL D. SCULL'S "THISTLE" COTTAGE.

THE PERSEVERANCE.

The brig Perseverance, from Havre, France, to New York, laden with a cargo valued at $400,000, was wrecked nearly opposite the point where the "Ocean Rest" now stands, in the month of December, 1815. The day previous to the disaster (Friday) a vessel from New York was spoken who told the Perseverance she was 200 miles east of Sandy Hook. The news occasioned great joy among the crew and passengers of whom there were seven of the former and ten of the latter, as they expected, according to this intelligence, to land in New York on the following day. The captain, imbued with the spirit engendered by the fatal error to a degree, of recklessness, spread every stitch of canvas to a heavy nor'easter and, with spars strained to their utmost, and cordage creaking, the good ship sped merrily on to her swift destruction. At 3 o'clock A.M. on Saturday the warning cry of breakers ahead was sounded, and a moment later the vessel struck, refused to obey her helm, and backed up on the beach stern foremost. In a short time the sea broke entirely over her. The wildest confusion prevailed as the passengers rushed from the cabin with no protection from a piercing storm of snow and hail but their night clothing. Eight of the seventeen souls on board got into the long boat and a heavy sea swept it overboard. It was then discovered to be fastened by a cable which they were unable to cut or in any way detach, and amid piercing shrieks, with the means of rescue just at hand, as the long boat would probably have floated to shore, they went down beside the vessel. The others succeeded in reaching the round-top except a Frenchman by the name of Cologne, who remained in the shrouds. At daybreak the vessel was discovered from the mainland, and willing hearts sped across the bay and down the beach to the rescue. Boats were launched again and again only to be capsized and hurled back by the angry waters. Every means which human skill and daring could devise was tried till Sunday at noon, when they signaled to the vessel that nothing more could be done, and they should try to build a raft of the spars. The poor wretches held up their pocket books and watches as an inducement for those on shore to continue their efforts, but the limit of their power had been reached long before. Exhaustion from cold and hunger now did rapid work, and one by one, until but five were left, they dropped into the sea. Captain Snow, one of the remaining five, attempted to swim ashore and was lost. In the meantime the mate, who had fortunately secured a hatchet, constructed a raft. A negro, who was assisting, was washed overboard, but swam to shore. The Frenchman, who had remained in the shrouds up till this time, fell into the water senseless; he was caught by the hair and thus towed behind the raft, which was finally carried ashore by the breakers. The saddest procession that ever trod this beach took up the line of march toward the bay to cross to the mainland. Four exhausted, half-frozen men, borne in the arms of those who had gone to the rescue, followed by others bearing a rudely constructed bier upon which lay the form of a young French girl, the only female on board the ill-fated vessel, and the only victim whose body floated to shore. Her linen clothing was daintily embroidered, and jewelry was concealed in the braids of her hair. Many reports were given of her beauty. Dr. Maurice Beasley, an eye-witness, said: "She was the concentration of all the graces of the female form." Her remains were interred in the burying ground of the Golden family, a little plot now overgrown with weeds and briars a short distance from the wharf at Beasley's Point. Three days later her uncle, Mr. Cologne, who died from exhaustion was buried by her side. For seven miles, the entire length of the island, the beach was strewn with cashmere shawls, leghorn flats, thread lace, fine china and bales of silk and satin. Remnants of the merchandise are still in existence. It is supposed the hull is lying some distance out, covered with sand, and still contains treasure. After the storm of September, 1889, which swept the Atlantic seaboard, pieces of china washed ashore at this point, which, when compared with those secured at the time of the wreck, are of the same design, pattern and quality, and are doubtless from the old brig. These tangible links thrown across nearly three-quarters of a century connecting us so closely with the Perseverance, tell of a time when Madison was president of the United States. The treaty of peace with Great Britain had just

REV. E. B. LAKE'S COTTAGE.

been signed. The little Clermont, or " Fulton's Folly," had but a short time before revealed the adaptation of a power that should revolutionize navigation; the magnetic telegraph was unknown till nearly thirty years later, and not till after fifty years had passed was the Atlantic cable completed.

J. AND H. SCULL.

The two-masted schooner J. and H. Scull, lumber laden, from a North Carolina port to Atlantic City, attempted to enter Great Egg Harbor Bay, and stranded, January 18, 1892. The vessel struck with great force. By the skillful management of the captain she cleared the bar and swept into deeper waters, only to become unmanageable and aground a second time. The life-guards of Ocean City Life-Saving station immediately signaled to her, and a little later the surf-boat was launched and speeding over the water. The muscle and brawn of powerful arms were brought into full play as the guards bent gallantly to the oars, while the voice of the captain rang above the roar and tumult of the waves, as he issued his orders, standing firm and erect in the stern of the boat, guiding it upon its perilous journey, one moment poised upon the crest of a wave and the next buried from the sight in the trough of the sea, to rise again on the succeeding wave. The work of transferring the crew from the vessel to the surf-boat was very dangerous, the heavy sea causing the vessel to plunge violently. The captain, the mate, two sailors, the cook and his wife were finally landed without any loss of life. All efforts to remove the vessel from the bar were ineffectual; she was then stripped of sails, cordage and topmasts, partially unloaded and abandoned for a time. The J. and H. Scull was an exceptionally staunch vessel. February 29th, during a violent storm, she cut through and displaced tons of the sand in which she was imbedded, plunged across the channel and landed on the main beach, without one bolt of her hull withdrawn, the mainmast and bowsprit intact, and the gilt arabesque scroll work of the figure head untarnished. Remains of the hull may now be seen at the north point of the beach.

PANCHITO.

Among the driftwood piled here and there on the island may be seen an occasional piece of logwood, which owes its preservation to the fact of its tough, hard fibre, being almost proof against destruction by ordinary tools. This wood, lying hundreds of miles from its native soil, was brought here by the Spanish brig, Panchito, wrecked February 13, 1888. The circumstances attending the disaster were very mysterious. She came on the bar in the night, but sent up no signals of distress, and even extinguished her lights. At daybreak the life-guards discovered the vessel lying in a dangerous position and immediately went to her aid. The captain represented her as belonging to a wealthy ranchman of Vera Cruz and bound for New York. The deck was loaded with logwood, and the hold was partly loaded with logwood and hides. The crew of thirteen men were taken off in life-boats and cared for at the life-saving station. After seven days of hard labor a wrecking steamer succeeded in getting the vessel off the bar. As she was being towed into deeper water the cable parted and she struck again. The deck load was thrown off and she floated a second time. A small quantity of hard tack, a few Mexican beans and a little sugar was all there was on board to eat. The first mate, an American, was intelligent and well educated. His log book was remarkable for neatness and beauty of penmanship. The captain and second mate were coarse and ignorant Spaniards. They were each armed with a pair of revolvers and a huge dirk. The latter was stuck inside the waistband on the left side in front, and was carried without any sheath. It was a constant source of wonder to spectators how this could be done without inflicting serious injury. The captain carried two watches of exquisite workmanship, besides a number of rings and other jewelry. The mates had in their posssession different kinds of jewelry set with precious stones. The ten sailors were a motley group indeed, and were in a filthy condition. Their long, unkempt hair, unshaven beards and swarthy complexions gave them the appearance of wild beasts rather than men. The weather was very cold, but they were without shoes or stockings, and their clothing was in every way insuffi-

REV. E. H. SANDERLIN'S COTTAGE.

cient. As soon as they landed they were fed and properly clothed. Four of them were Italians, one an immense negro, intensely black, from Yucatan, one a native of Manilla (southeast of China), one a Portuguese, two native Spaniards and two Mexicans completed the group. They all spoke Spanish. They were evidently unwilling to board the vessel the second time. As they stepped on deck the officers issued orders with dirk in hand, as if prepared to spring upon them at any moment. The vessel was towed to Philadelphia and was there abandoned by the sailors.

THE RHINE.

Over forty years ago, the Rhine, a full-rigged ship, went down near Corson's Inlet. She was carrying three hundred German emigrants to New York, beside a cargo of iron. All were saved but one child. Tents were pitched at the southern point of beach, where they were fed and sheltered until sent away by rail.

THE ELIZABETH.

Thirty years ago the full-rigged ship Elizabeth, Queenstown to New York, carrying two hundred and fifty Irish emigrants and a cargo of marble and cork, sank near Corson's Inlet. No lives were lost. The crew and passengers were taken to the Dolphin Hotel at Somers' Point. The following morning they were conveyed to the nearest railroad station to finish their journey by land, their numbers reinforced by several children born during the night. The old hotels could tell strange tales of shipwrecks ; how it was necessary at times to resort to severe measures to prevent bloodshed among the rescued crew and officers ; when the captain was secured with bolts in one room, the mates in another and the sailors imprisoned in still another apartment till their fury had subsided or they were removed to safer quarters. These troubles arose when the sailors, in mutiny, had wrecked the vessel purposely ; when the accident had occurred through the neglect of the officer on watch or the captain had been harsh and cruel.

WRECK IN THE BAY.

The long, low hull, lying keel upwards on Bond's Bar in Great Egg Harbor Bay, adds one more to the vast number of unknown wrecks which are cast up every year. This was first seen on Great Egg Harbor Bar, where it remained for a short time. During a storm it cleared the obstruction, and in the most uncanny manner wound its way in and out among the channels of the inlet as if guided by an unseen helmsman, never touching shoal or shore until it stranded on an island five miles from where it was first seen. It has been a well built copper-sheathed and bolted barkentine, bore a German name, and had been loaded with petroleum. The silent evidence of the most appalling of disasters, "burned at sea," tells the cause of shipwreck. A little more than a year previous to the time it was seen on this coast a vessel of the same name and cargo, in every way answering the description, was burned in the Mediterranean Sea. The hull drifted out through the straits of Gibralter and disappeared. It was several times reported, always in the same position—up-side down. It is the popular opinion of the coast guard of that body of water that this is the same wreck; that it has drifted with the ocean currents and been driven by storms till it has reached the point where it now lies.

Lack of space forbids an account of many other noted wrecks, among them the John Bentley, Utah, G. L. Thorn, Lottie Clotts, John Douglass, Caroline Hall, Zetland, Angela Brewer, Sallie Clark, Dashaway and Lawrence.

S. E. SAMUSON'S RESIDENCE.

Atlantic·Coast·Steamboat·Co.

TIME TABLE IN EFFECT JUNE 24, 1892.

LEAVE OCEAN CITY, SECOND STREET PIER.

Ocean City to Somers' Point, connecting for Pleasantville, May's Landing and Philadelphia—6.45, 8.10, 10.00, 11.00 A.M., 12.00 M., 2.15, 3.20, 4.20, 6.50, *7.10 P.M.

Somers' Point to Ocean City—*6.15, 8.00, 9.23, 10.45, 11.30 A.M., 2.00, 2.45, 3.45, 5.55, 11.50 P.M.

Ocean City to Longport, connecting for Atlantic City—*6.40, 7.20, 7.50, 8.25, 9.00, 9.40, 10.00, 10.45, 11.17, 11.35 A.M., 12.00 M., 1.25, 2.00, 2.30, 3.00, 3.20, 4.00, 4.45, 5.30, 6.50, 7.10 P.M.

Longport to Ocean City, upon arrival of trains from Atlantic City—7.05, 7.42, 8.15, 8.50, 9.23, 10.00, 10.30, 11.05, 11.40 A.M., 12.15, 12.45, 1.50, 2.20, 2.55, 3.25, 4.00, 4.35, 5.10, 6.00, *6.45, 7.30 P.M.

* Fishing boat daily.

Boats are run to connect with all trains.

EXCURSIONS TO SEA.

Hourly pleasure trips to sea are made by boats of this Company from the Pavilion at the Inlet at Atlantic City. They are also for charter for towing or special fishing, or Moonlight Excursions.

W. T. BARBER, Manager.

West·Jersey·Railroad.

FOR SEA ISLE CITY AND OCEAN CITY.

LEAVE PHILADELPHIA.

Express	9.10 A.M.	Express	4.20 P.M.
Accommodation	8.20 A.M.	Express	2.30 P.M.
Excursion	7.00 A.M.	Accommodation	3.40 P.M.

SUNDAYS.

Accommodation	7.10 A.M.	Express	8.50 A.M.
Excursion	7.00 A.M.		

LEAVE OCEAN CITY—Second Street.

Express	6.27 A.M.	Accommodation	1.53 P.M.
Accommodation	6.18 A.M.	Excursion	4.50 P.M.
Accommodation	9.43 A.M.	Express	5.00 P.M.

SUNDAYS.

Accommodation	3.35 P.M.	Excursion	5.42 P.M.
Express	5.22 P.M.	Accommodation	8.48 P.M.

Central Ave., Sea Isle City, and Thirty-fourth St., Ocean City, flag stations for all trains.

CHAS. E. PUGH, *Gen'l Manager.*   A. O. DAYTON, *Superintendent.*

F. P. CANFIELD,

Real Estate Agent.

Houses and Lots for sale in all parts of the city on easy terms.

There never will be a time when lots will be cheaper, with so many attractions as Ocean City offers, than now.

If you want a cottage or home by the sea, on one of the highest beaches on the New Jersey coast, with Great Egg Harbor Bay and Inlet on one side, and the Atlantic Ocean on the other, where the liquor traffic is prohibited in every deed, where the Sabbath is observed, where the grass and flowers grow with rare beauty, where the sailing is the finest and the boating safe as on an inland lake, where the bathing is as good at one hour of the day as another, and no life lines are needed, where there is one of the best boardwalks on the New Jersey coast along the strand, where there has not been a case of drowning in seven years, where but two persons have been arrested for disorderly conduct in eight years, where there is absolutely no malaria, where living expenses are as cheap as anywhere, where there is no healthier climate in America, then buy one or more lots at Ocean City, while they will cost but a fraction of what they are worth at other seaside resorts.

I have lots on the main avenues for sale at from $100 to $1000 each.

I am thoroughly conversant with all facts connected with property on the beach. Those desiring any information in regard to Ocean City, or about property, should call or correspond with me.

W. Cor. Sixth Street and Asbury Avenue,

OCEAN CITY, N. J.

4

Ocean City Sentinel

OCEAN CITY, NEW JERSEY.

R. CURTIS ROBINSON, Editor and Prop'r.

A spicy seven-column sheet, with a very large circulation. Published on the border and circulates in three adjoining counties, as well as nearly every state of the Union. Advertisers will be wise in giving the SENTINEL a trial order, as our city is visited by thousands from a distance. Rates reasonable. Published every Thursday.

A Moral Seaside Resort.

Not excelled as a Health Restorer

FINEST FACILITIES FOR

FISHING, SAILING, GUNNING, ETC.

Ocean City.

EVERY LOVER OF

TEMPERANCE AND MORALS

SHOULD COMBINE TO HELP US.

THOUSANDS OF LOTS FOR SALE AT VARIOUS PRICES,
LOCATED IN ALL PARTS OF THE CITY.

Apply to Superintendent,

E. B. LAKE.

FINELY EQUIPPED. CUISINE EXCELLENT. OPEN ALL THE YEAR.

ALL MODERN IMPROVEMENTS—STEAM HEAT, GAS, ETC.

J. T. ADAMS, Prop.,

The Traymore,

COR. NINTH AND WESLEY AVENUE.

RATES, $2.00 TO $2.50 PER DAY. SPECIAL
RATES FOR SEASON.

✳ THE ✳

Allaire Cottage,

Cor. Sixth St. and Central Ave.

Delightfully located between the bay and the ocean. The well-known reputation of this house will be fully sustained during the present season.

MRS. A. B. RANCK, Proprietress.

Bishop Foster's Heresy,

By REV. JAMES E. LAKE, B.D., of the N. J. Conference,

KEYPORT, N. J.

"A sharp book."—*Camden Post.* "Written with marked ability."—*Dr. Deems.*

212 pages. Sent on receipt of price, postpaid, $1.00.

PLASTERERS AND BRICKLAYERS.

W. STONEHILL.   C. O. ADAMS.

STONEHILL & ADAMS,

Plastering, Range Setting, Bricklaying, &c.

ALL WORK IN MASON LINE PROMPTLY ATTENDED TO.

OCEAN CITY, N. J.

HARRY L. CONVER,

Fine Cigars & Tobacco, Full Line of Pipes & Smoking Tobacco

FIRST-CLASS BARBER SHOP.

LADIES' HAIR CUTTING AND SHAMPOOING A SPECIALTY.

711 ASBURY AVENUE.

King's American Laundry,

ASBURY AVENUE BELOW FOURTH STREET, OCEAN CITY, N. J.

Shirts	.10	Flannels .... .50 a suit
Collars	.03	Ladies' White Dresses 1.00
Cuffs	.04	Ladies' Gingham .... .50
White Vests	.25	Wrappers .... .25
Gents' Underwear	.08 a piece	White Skirts .... .25
Gents' Hose	.05 a piece	Washing .... 1.00 per doz.

ALL WORK DONE IN FIRST-CLASS STYLE.

MRS. ANNA KING, Proprietress.

Ocean City House

OCEAN CITY, N. J.,

Asbury Avenue, between Seventh and Eighth Streets,

MRS. J. T. PRICE, -   -   PROPRIETRESS.

Pleasantly located. Convenient to R. R. station and Post Office. Terms moderate. Open all the year.

J. S. RUSH,

House and Sign Painter

FRESCOING AND HARD-
WOOD FINISHING.

JOBBING A SPECIALTY.

ESTIMATES FURNISHED

On all kinds of work.

ORDERS FROM A DISTANCE FILLED PROMPTLY.

OCEAN CITY, N. J.